Amazing
Frogs & Toads

EYEWITNESS JUNIORS

Amazing
Frogs & Toads

WRITTEN BY
BARRY CLARKE

PHOTOGRAPHED BY
JERRY YOUNG

ALFRED A. KNOPF • NEW YORK

Conceived and produced by
Dorling Kindersley Limited

Project editors Helen Parker and Christine Webb
Art editor Ann Cannings
Managing editor Sophie Mitchell
Editorial director Sue Unstead
Art director Colin Walton

Special photography by Jerry Young
and Jane Burton (page 28)
Illustrations by Ruth Lindsay, Polly Noakes,
and John Hutchinson
Animals supplied by Trevor Smith's Animal World
Editorial consultants The staff of the Natural History Museum, London

This is a Borzoi Book published by Alfred A. Knopf, Inc.

First American edition, 1990

Manufactured in Italy   0 9 8 7 6 5 4

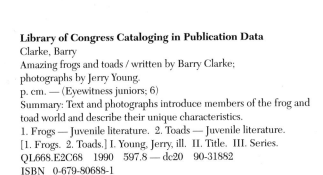

Library of Congress Cataloging in Publication Data
Clarke, Barry
Amazing frogs and toads / written by Barry Clarke;
photographs by Jerry Young.
p. cm. — (Eyewitness juniors; 6)
Summary: Text and photographs introduce members of the frog and
toad world and describe their unique characteristics.
1. Frogs — Juvenile literature. 2. Toads — Juvenile literature.
[1. Frogs. 2. Toads.] I. Young, Jerry, ill. II. Title. III. Series.
QL668.E2C68 1990   597.8 — dc20   90-31882
ISBN   0-679-80688-1
ISBN   0-679-90688-6 (lib. bdg.)

Color reproduction by Colourscan, Singapore
Typeset by Windsorgraphics, Ringwood, Hampshire
Printed in Italy by A. Mondadori Editore, Verona

Contents

What is a frog?

Frogs and toads have short, round bodies and large heads with bulging eyes. They have no tail, no fur, feathers, or scales, and no neck. They are amphibians (am-FIB-ee-uns), which means they can live on land or in water.

skull

arm

four fingers

leg

five toes

lungs

heart

Amphibians
Frogs and toads are not the only kinds of amphibian. There are also newts and salamanders, which have long tails, and caecilians (see-SILL-ee-uns), which look like big worms.

Newt

Salamander

Caecilian

Most frogs and toads have big eyes so they can see their food – and their enemies!

Breathing
Like you, frogs have lungs for breathing. But unlike you, they can also breathe through their skin.

Beneath the skin
Frogs have short front legs, long back legs for jumping, and webbed feet for swimming.

This frog has smooth, moist skin

8

Neat feet

Frogs have different feet for different lifestyles. Some have pointed toes, some have sticky toes for climbing, and others have webbed toes for swimming.

digging   climbing   swimming

The oldest singer in town

Insects made the first noises, but the first true song was probably sung by a prehistoric frog.

New discoveries

Many new kinds of frog are found every year. Until 1980 no one knew this little Majorcan midwife toad existed!

Bright eyes

The colored part of a frog's eye is called the iris (EYE-riss). It can be deep red, brown, black, green, silver, bronze, or gold. The dark center, or pupil, isn't always round like a human's. Some are triangular; others are heart-shaped.

This toad has dryish, warty skin

Frog or toad?

Frogs usually have smooth, moist skin. Toads are more stout and most of them have drier, warty skins. But they are really all frogs.

Frogs in water

Most frogs live both on land and in water. But some frogs spend their whole lives in the water. These are truly aquatic frogs.

Flat frog
The Chilean aquatic bullfrog has a floppy body and long legs – just right for swimming.

Frog expert
Reading this book is the easy way to learn about frogs. A frog expert, or herpetologist (HER-puh-TAHL-uh-jist), spends hours watching and waiting by ponds and lakes, in all kinds of weather.

Hairy frogs?
The "hairs" on this male frog's body are really tiny folds of skin. They help it breathe more easily when it is darting around during the breeding season.

Chilean aquatic bullfrog
This massive frog spends most of its life in rivers and lakes. It is so greedy it even tries to eat animals nearly as big as itself!

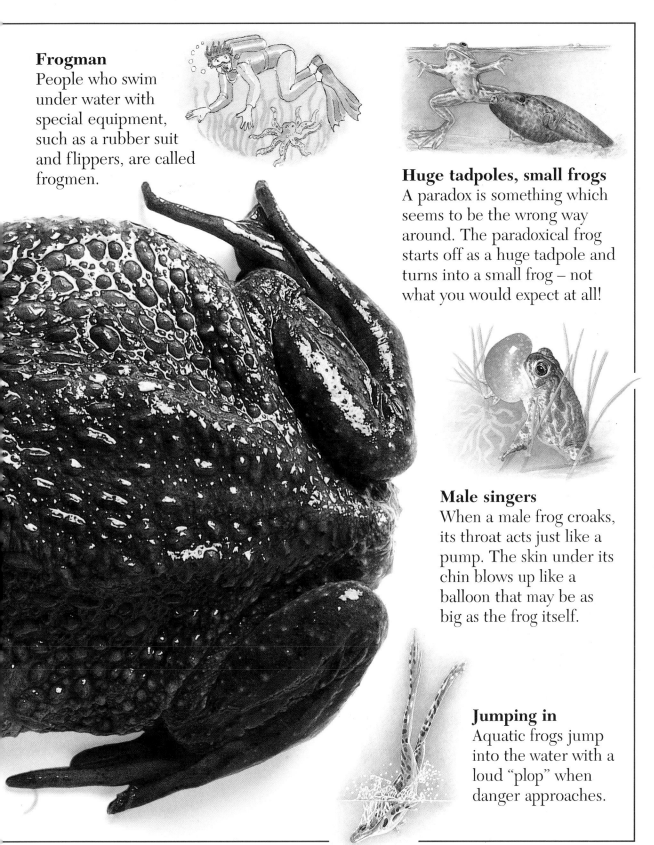

Frogman
People who swim under water with special equipment, such as a rubber suit and flippers, are called frogmen.

Huge tadpoles, small frogs
A paradox is something which seems to be the wrong way around. The paradoxical frog starts off as a huge tadpole and turns into a small frog – not what you would expect at all!

Male singers
When a male frog croaks, its throat acts just like a pump. The skin under its chin blows up like a balloon that may be as big as the frog itself.

Jumping in
Aquatic frogs jump into the water with a loud "plop" when danger approaches.

Burrowing frogs

For many frogs, life is safer under the ground than above. Here they can hide from hungry enemies but still find plenty to eat. Many frogs, like this narrow-mouthed toad from Malaysia, are master burrowers.

Stony-faced
Sitting on the leafy forest floor, this little toad looks just like a slimy wet stone.

Bottom first...
This holy cross toad has a strange way of digging. It shuffles its back legs and then uses the "spades" on its back feet to clear away the soil. Once it has buried itself, it peeks above the ground to spot a passing meal.

Head first...
Some frogs have hard, sharp snouts which they use for burrowing. This frog pushes its snout into the ground, like a shovel. Then it uses its front legs to dig in – head first.

...Feet last
The spades on the back feet help push the frog's snout into the ground – until it disappears.

Rain frogs

These frogs usually see the light of day only in the rainy season. They spend most of their time in underground tunnels or beneath logs – often sharing their homes with scorpions.

Digging with their bare hands

This natterjack toad doesn't need a spade for digging in the sand. His short, stubby fingers with hard tips do the job.

Short, strong back legs for burrowing into the soil – bottom first

The mouse, the frog, and the hawk

An old story tells how a frog and a mouse tie their feet together as a sign of friendship. At lunch-time, the frog leaps into the pond to eat and drowns the poor mouse. The mouse's body floats to the top of the water and is soon spotted by a hungry hawk, who picks it up and flies off with a double dinner.

Life in the treetops

Some tree frogs spend their whole lives in the trees, never coming down to the ground. They eat, sleep, find a mate, and even lay their eggs up in the branches or on leaves.

Fighting in the trees

A tree frog's home is its castle. And it is not afraid to fight for its own leaf, branch, or fallen log.

big eyes to look out for food – and danger

sticky pads for clinging on

Sunbathing frogs

Frogs need to protect their skin from the sun, just as we do. This South American frog makes a waxy, fatty lotion and wipes it all over its body.

Weather forecast

In Germany, people used to keep green tree frogs in jars with a ladder and some water. When the frogs climbed the ladder, it meant the weather would change. But the poor frogs probably just wanted to get out of the jars!

Sticky feet
Tree frogs have sticky pads on their fingers and toes to help them climb on slippery leaves.

Tree frogs can climb up glass

High jumper
To make sure they land on the right leaf, flying frogs steer in the air with their webbed hands and feet.

Red-eyed tree frog
This Central American frog lays its eggs under leaves that hang over water. As they hatch out, the tadpoles fall into the water below.

Singing in the trees
This Mexican tree frog (right) is singing to his mate – hoping that she will come to his leafy home.

All fingers and toes

As well as living in trees, some tree frogs live in bushes, reeds, and long grass. They climb from leaf to leaf, hanging on with their sticky fingers and toes.

Spring is here!
The tinkling song of the spring peeper is one of the first signs of spring in parts of North America.

Home lovers
In Australia, White's tree frogs often share people's bathrooms.

See-through
The glass frog has strange see-through skin. You can even see this one's heart and insides.

Foam-nesting frogs
Some female tree frogs make a kind of egg white. They beat it into a foam with their back legs and lay their eggs in it. This bubbly nest is dry on the outside but moist inside, where the eggs are.

Leaf-folding frogs
This golden frog lays its eggs on leaves in the water. Then it folds and glues the leaves together to hide the eggs.

Baby-sitting
Male glass frogs watch carefully over their eggs to keep them from being eaten by other animals. They often rest a hand on the edge of the pile of eggs, though no one really knows why.

White's tree frog
This little Australian frog seems at home on its tree branch. But it doesn't mind visiting people in their homes, either.

Foam birth
When the rains come, the foam-nesting frog's nest becomes runny. The rain water – and the tadpoles – drip into the water below.

Big mouth, big appetite

Frogs don't eat three meals a day as we do. They eat a lot of food when there's a lot to eat, and they can go for a long time between meals. If they can eat, they will – their next meal might be a long way away!

A frog blinks as it swallows – its eyeballs help force the food down

Sticky tongue
Many frogs and toads have sticky tongues which they can flick out to catch their prey.

Once it has pulled an insect into its mouth, the frog doesn't stop to chew, but swallows its meal whole.

Chinese eclipse
We now know that eclipses of the moon are caused by the shadow of the earth falling on the moon. But the Chinese once believed they were caused by a three-legged frog who swallowed the moon.

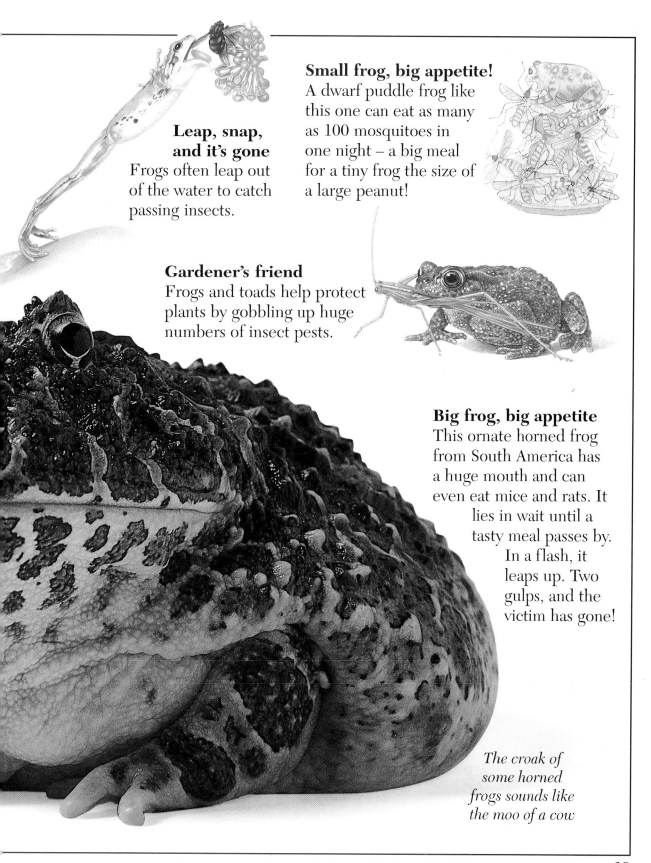

Leap, snap, and it's gone
Frogs often leap out of the water to catch passing insects.

Small frog, big appetite!
A dwarf puddle frog like this one can eat as many as 100 mosquitoes in one night – a big meal for a tiny frog the size of a large peanut!

Gardener's friend
Frogs and toads help protect plants by gobbling up huge numbers of insect pests.

Big frog, big appetite
This ornate horned frog from South America has a huge mouth and can even eat mice and rats. It lies in wait until a tasty meal passes by. In a flash, it leaps up. Two gulps, and the victim has gone!

The croak of some horned frogs sounds like the moo of a cow

Not too hot, not too cold

Frogs are cold-blooded, which means that their inside temperature is about the same as the temperature outside. They keep warm by sitting in the sun, and go into the shade or the water to cool off.

A fully grown African bullfrog might be as big as a football

Dry-weather coat
The African bullfrog digs in underground. It wraps itself in a cocoon, like a papery overcoat, made from old skin. This cocoon keeps the frog from drying out when the weather is hot. When the rains come, they seep down, waking up the frog.

Feet in, head down...

If a frog gets hot, it may tuck in its arms, hands, and feet to keep them cool. Oddly enough, it does the same thing in cold weather – this time to keep warm.

Singing in the rain

In hot countries, frogs breed in the rainy season. As soon as the rains begin, the male frogs start croaking wildly to attract partners.

Freezing frogs!

Four kinds of frog can survive the freezing cold of a Canadian winter. They become covered in a blanket of ice, their hearts stop beating, and they even stop breathing.

Water-holding frog

This frog lives in the hot Australian deserts, where it hardly rains. It can store large amounts of water in its body.

Wake me when it's warmer...

Many frogs escape the worst of the winter by hiding under a log or in the mud at the bottom of a pond. Then they go into a kind of deep sleep until spring.

...or when it's colder

In hot countries, frogs stay out of the heat. Some may sleep underground all summer, until the rains arrive.

How not to be eaten

Frogs make a tasty meal for many animals. To protect themselves from being eaten, they can hide, pretend to be fierce or frightening, or make poisons in their skin so that they taste bad.

Water babies
Frogs that live in puddles, ponds, lakes, and streams often leave only the tops of their heads and eyes showing. If they sense danger, they dive for safety.

Hidden near to a log or stone, this toad is hard to see – until it moves

In hiding
Some frogs blend in perfectly with their surroundings, like this one on its lily pad home.

On tiptoe
A snake could easily gobble up this toad. To frighten it off, the toad puffs itself up and stands on tiptoe so it looks twice as big.

Poison glands

Some toads, like the cane toad, make poison in glands behind their eyes. If a dog tried to pick up the toad, its poison could squirt into the dog's mouth. This would make the dog very ill – it could even die.

Deadly yellow

This dart-poison or arrow-poison frog is so poisonous that it shouldn't be touched. One frog's poison can kill 20,000 mice.

Poison pipes

South American Indians use the arrow-poison frog's poison for hunting. They put it on the darts for their blowpipes.

Green toads hide during the day and come out at night

I'm an owl, and I could eat YOU!

When it is threatened the false-eyed frog hunches over to show two eyespots. To put off braver enemies, a foul-smelling liquid oozes out around the eyespots. If the eyes don't work, the smell should do it!

Green toad

This handsome toad can puff itself up with air to look bigger and frighten its enemies.

Hop, skip, and a jump

Frogs can leap away from trouble.

Curious colors

Don't be fooled!
This dart-poison frog looks like a strawberry – but its skin is poisonous.

Not *all* frogs are dull brown or grassy green. There are yellow, orange, gold, red, white, and even blue frogs, and some of them are beautifully patterned with many bright colors.

Warning! You can't eat me!
Bright colors, especially yellows and reds, warn other animals that a frog tastes bad or is poisonous. The poison in the skin of these little dart-poison frogs could kill you.

Feeling blue
Some male frogs turn blue to attract a female. But this beautiful blue dart-poison frog has a brilliant blue and black pattern all year round.

The tips of the fingers and toes look as if they have been dipped in a can of red paint

Hidden away

Soldiers wear green and brown clothes so their enemies cannot see them in the fields and forests. This type of clothing is called camouflage.

Now you see me, now you don't

This striped frog from South Africa would easily be seen away from the reeds and tall grasses where it lives. Put it back in its home and it is almost impossible to find.

Light and shade

This little African frog looks just like part of the grass it is sitting on. The light and dark stripes that run down its body match the striped patterns made by sunlight falling on its reedy home.

wide stripe

narrow stripe

Split in two!

The light lines running down the backs of these two puddle frogs break up their round body shape and make them harder to see.

Tricky toad

From above, the Oriental fire-bellied toad from China (left) blends in with its leafy background. But when it is disturbed, it arches its back and flashes the bottoms of its colorful feet. This quickly scares off hungry enemies.

Strange shapes

Not all frogs look like frogs. Some are shaped like leaves, others have small heads, and still others have heads that look like a duck's bill. Their unusual shapes help the frogs survive wherever they may live.

Big leaf frogs
The Asian leaf frog has flaps of skin (or "horns") over its eyes, and a pointed snout. Its brown skin and jagged shape make it look just like dried leaves on the forest floor.

Helmet head!
This frog's unusual shape helps it blend in with its surroundings. Its oddly shaped head – prongs at the back, a pointed nose, and a very bony skull – looks like a helmet.

Mole frog

Mole

Mole or frog?
The Australian mole frog lives in sandy places and in termite mounds. It looks like a mole, with its small head, tiny eyes, and rounded snout. It even digs like a mole – head first, using its strong arms.

World on his shoulders
People from China and India once believed that the world rested on the back of a giant three-legged frog. But if the frog made the slightest move, it would cause an earthquake.

A duck-billed frog?
The Mexican spoon-headed frog backs into holes in logs and trees. Its bony head fits tightly into the hole, like a cork. This makes it a lot harder for animals to pull it out and make a meal of it.

Little leaf frogs
This little Darwin's frog, with its pointed snout, looks like a green leaf. Having both the right color and body shape keeps it extra safe.

Frogs and tadpoles

Frogs begin life as eggs. When the eggs hatch, tadpoles swim out. Then the tadpoles slowly turn into small frogs. This amazing change is called metamorphosis (MET-uh-MOR-fuh-siss).

1 When a tadpole hatches out of its egg (or frog spawn), it has a round head and body, and a tail. But it has no legs.

2 The tadpole's back legs appear later. It swims using its tail and little back legs.

3 Next, its front legs pop out. As it feeds, the tadpole's body starts to grow.

4 As its body grows, the four-legged tadpole's tail gets smaller and smaller. It is now a froglet.

5 At last the tadpole has become a tiny frog. It is just like its mother, only much smaller.

Frogs in the throat...

The male Darwin's frog swallows its tadpoles into a kind of throat pouch. When the tadpoles become froglets, he spits them out, one by one.

..and in the stomach

The stomach-brooding frog swallows her eggs or tadpoles into her stomach. When they turn into froglets, they leave via Mom's mouth!

Nurse frogs

When their tadpoles hatch, arrow-poison frogs carry them on their backs to their nursery pool.

Caring dads

Male midwife toads carry their strings of eggs wrapped around their back legs.

Frogs with pockets

The male hip-pocket frog carries its tadpoles in pouches – one on each side of its body.

On their backs

Some female toads carry their sticky eggs on the spongy skin on their backs.